Favorite
Fables
of
Aesop

Collected By
Judith Pasamanick

Illustrated by
Anita Nelson

Modern Curriculum Press

ACKNOWLEDGMENTS

"The Fox and the Crow" by James Thurber, copyright © 1956 by James Thurber, © 1984 by Helen Thurber. From FURTHER FABLES FOR OUR TIME, published by Simon & Schuster.

Every reasonable effort has been made to locate the ownership of copyrighted materials and to make due acknowledgment. Any errors or omissions will gladly be rectified in future editions.

Design: Ade Skunta and Company
Project Editor: Marty Geyen
Associate Editor: Mary Ann Porrata

ISBN 0-8136-2401-0

10 9 8 7 6 5 4 3 2 1   93 92 91 90

Who Was Aesop?

Aesop was a storyteller who lived in Greece over 2,500 years ago. No one knows very much about Aesop's life. It is believed that he was a slave to a rich man, who set him free because Aesop was so wise and clever. Later, it is thought, he was the advisor to a king and was very much respected.

It is also thought that Aesop was not very handsome, but that he had something more important than good looks. He had wit, common sense, and humor. He told stories that made a point and he used them to solve problems. The stories that Aesop told are called *fables*. They were passed from one person to another and were not written down until hundreds of years later.

What are fables? They are short stories about people and animals that say things about the way people act toward one another. It takes a lot of thought to understand a fable. That is because there is a story behind every story in a fable. If you work at it, you will see things in the fables that are like things that happen in your own life. Who knows? Maybe these stories will make you want to write your own fable.

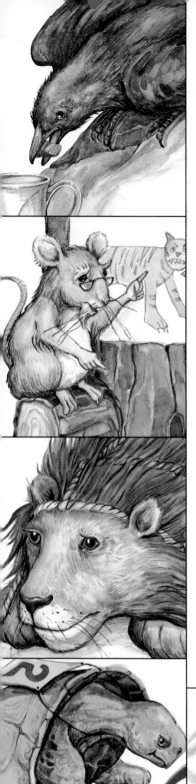

Table of Contents

Introduction   3

The Crow and the Pitcher   6

Belling the Cat   8

The Lion and the Mouse   10

The Tortoise and the Hare   12

The Wind and the Sun   14

The Oak and the Reed   16

The Town Mouse and the
Country Mouse   18

The Miller, the Boy, and
the Donkey   20

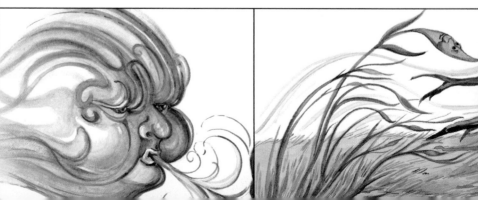

Two Travelers and an Axe   22

The Fox and the Stork   24

The Wolf and the Crane   26

The Shepherd Who Cried ''Wolf!''   28

The Fox and the Grapes   29

The Fox and the Crow   30
(Aesop)

The Fox and the Crow   32
(James Thurber)

This fable tells about a crow's problem
and the clever way he solves it.

The Crow and the Pitcher

One day a crow was looking for water. It was
very hot and the crow wanted water very much.
He felt sick. If he did not find water soon,
he thought that he would die.

Then he came to a pitcher and looked in.
He saw some water, but it was so far down he
couldn't reach it. He tried and tried to get a
sip, but at last he had to give up.

Then the crow looked down and saw some
pebbles nearby. He had an idea! He took
a pebble and dropped it
into the pitcher.

Then he took *another* pebble
and dropped it into the pitcher.

Then he took *another* pebble
and dropped it into the pitcher.

Then he took *yet another*
pebble and dropped it into
the pitcher.

Slowly the water began to rise higher and higher. The crow dropped a few more pebbles into the pitcher. *Now* he could drink the water. *It tasted so good.* He could drink all the water he wanted. That's how the crow saved his own life.

Little by little does the trick.

This fable tells about some mice with a problem and how important it was for them to solve it. Maybe you can help them.

Belling the Cat

Long ago a group of mice held a meeting. They wanted to decide what to do about their enemy the cat. Some mice wanted to try one plan and some called for another. At last a young mouse got up and said that he had an idea.

"Our biggest problem," he said, "is that the cat walks so quietly. We do not hear her coming, so she surprises us. My idea is to get a small bell. We could tie it around the cat's neck. Then we could hear her coming and we can get out of the way."

All of the other mice thought the idea was wonderful. Then an old mouse stood up and said, "This idea may sound good, but it also gives us another problem. *Who will bell the cat?*"

The mice all looked at one another. No one spoke. Then all the mice nodded their heads and said, "Indeed, who *will* bell the cat?"

Easier said than done.

The two animals in this fable are very different but they have the same problem. Discover what it is.

The Lion and the Mouse

Once a lion was fast asleep in his den. Suddenly, a little mouse ran over his nose and woke him. The mighty lion clapped his huge paw over the tiny mouse and opened his jaws W-I-D-E to eat him.

"I'm sorry, O King of the Forest," squeaked the mouse. "Please do not eat me! A mouse is not a meal for a lion. Spare me and I will never run up and down on you again. Who knows? Perhaps I can even help you some day."

The lion smiled. How could such a little animal ever help him? What a funny idea! He laughed and laughed and let the mouse go.

10

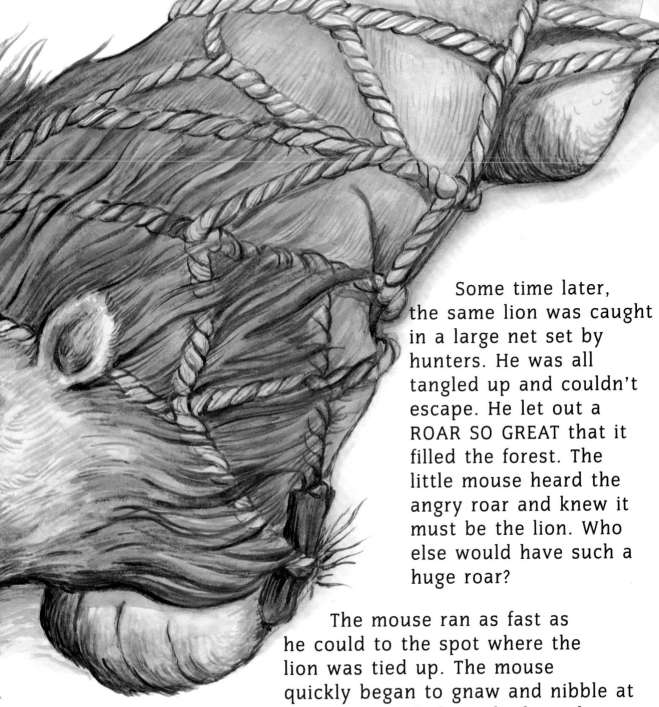

Some time later, the same lion was caught in a large net set by hunters. He was all tangled up and couldn't escape. He let out a ROAR SO GREAT that it filled the forest. The little mouse heard the angry roar and knew it must be the lion. Who else would have such a huge roar?

The mouse ran as fast as he could to the spot where the lion was tied up. The mouse quickly began to gnaw and nibble at the net. He bit and chewed, chewed and bit until—at last—the lion was free!

"You see," said the mouse, "I was right. Even a little mouse like me can help a mighty lion like you."

One good turn deserves another.   11

You may have heard this
fable before. As you read,
think about how this fable
is a little like the story
of *The Lion and the Mouse*.

The Tortoise and the Hare

One day the hare was bragging
to the other animals about how
fast he could run. He said, "When
I run as fast as I can, no one can beat me.
I dare any one of you here to race with me."

No one spoke. Then the tortoise said
quietly, "I will race with you."

"You must be joking," said the hare. "I could
dance around you all the way and still win."

"Don't brag until you have won," answered
the tortoise. "Shall we begin?" The hare agreed.

The hare ran very fast at first, but soon he stopped.
"Why am I running so fast?" he thought. "The tortoise
is far behind me. He will never win. Besides, the sun
is so hot today and that leafy tree can give me shade.
I will just lie down and take a little nap."
So that is just what he did.

Meanwhile, the tortoise kept walking on and on.
Soon he came to where the hare lay sleeping in the grass.
The tortoise smiled to himself. "Just as I thought," he said

and kept right on going. He walked and he walked and he didn't stop even once.

When the hare woke up, he stretched and yawned and looked around. "Ho, hum," he said, "I wonder where that slow old tortoise is by now?" He looked back down the road, but he didn't see the tortoise there. He looked ahead and there was the tortoise, almost at the end of the race.

"Oh, no!" cried the hare. He jumped up and ran as fast as he could, but he was not fast enough. The tortoise reached the finish line first. Then he turned to the hare and said, "Slow but steady wins the race."

Slow but steady wins the race.

The next two fables are alike in a special way.
See if you can figure out how they are alike.

The Wind and the Sun

One day the wind and the sun were having an argument.
"I am stronger than you are," said the wind.
"You think so?" said the sun.

"Yes," said the wind. "I can blow hard and make trees bend. I can make a lot of noise, but you are very quiet. You just sit there. Besides, I am much stronger than you are. You are really very weak."

"We'll see," said the sun. "Let's have a contest. Then we will find out for sure who is stronger." The wind agreed.

14

"Do you see that man down there?" asked the sun. The wind looked down and saw a man walking along the road. "Let's see which one of us can make that man take off his coat," said the sun.

"Oh, that will be easy," said the wind.

"You go first," said the sun as it hid behind a cloud to watch.

The wind began to blow on the man. So the man pulled his coat closer around him. The wind blew harder and harder. Still the man did not take off his coat. The wind blew again as hard as it could. The harder the wind blew, the more the man shivered and pulled his coat around him.

At last the wind said, "I have done all I can, but I can't blow his coat off. I give up."

Then the sun took its turn. It peeked from behind the cloud and began to shine kindly on the man. The man began to feel warm. He smiled. The sun felt so good after that cold, raw wind.

The sun shone brighter and brighter. The man opened his coat. The sun beamed and beamed and the man got warmer and warmer. Finally, he felt so hot that he had to take off his coat.

The sun turned to the wind. "You see," said the sun. "You will get more with kindness than with force."

You will get more with kindness than with force.

The Oak and the Reed

A tall oak looked down at a slim reed that was growing at its feet. "Well, small reed," said the oak, "why aren't you more like me? Look. My feet go deep into the ground. I hold my head high in the air. I am much stronger than you are!"

"True," said the reed. "I am not as big as you are. Still, being big does not always make you safe. I think I am *safer* than you are."

"Safer!" laughed the oak. "I am safer than you. Who could pick *me* up by the roots or push *my* head into the ground?"

"We will see," said the reed quietly.

Soon the oak was sorry for its words. A terrible wind began to blow. The oak stood proudly against it, but it was a very strong wind. The wind was so strong it lifted the tall oak, roots and all, out of the ground. Then it tossed that mighty tree into the river!

When the same strong wind blew the slim reed, it just bent over. When the wind stopped blowing, the reed stood up straight again as it had before.

It is better to bend than to break.

Have you heard the saying, *Different strokes for different folks?* What do you suppose it means? Read this fable and find out.

The Town Mouse and the Country Mouse

A town mouse once went to visit his friend in the country. The country mouse was very glad to see the town mouse. He ran around finding the best food that he could for his friend. He scurried here and there and finally found a few peas, bits of barley, scraps of cheese, and some nuts and grains. The food was not fancy but it was all he had to offer.

When the town mouse saw the country food he turned up his long nose. "Why, you eat like an *ant* here!" he said, laughing at his friend. "I can't understand how you put up with such poor food. I suppose you can't expect anything better here in the country."

Then the town mouse had an idea. "Come with me to the town for just one week," he said. "You will love life in the town. You will never want to come back to the country again."

No sooner said than done. The two mice set off for the town. They arrived at the home of the town mouse very late at night.

"You must be tired after our long trip," said the town mouse. "Would you like something to eat?"

The town mouse took his friend into the grand dining room. There they found what was left of a fine feast. They saw bags full of barley, thick chunks of cheddar cheese, pots of honey, and baskets full of dates. For dessert, they dined on cakes and jellies.

Suddenly they heard some loud growling and barking! "What's that?" cried the country mouse trembling in fear.

"Only the dogs of the house coming in with their masters," said the town mouse.

"Only dogs!" squeaked the country mouse, terribly, terribly scared. "I do not like *that* kind of music."

Just at that moment, the door flew open and two huge dogs charged in. The two mice ran as fast as they could and hid in a far corner. As soon as they were safe, the country mouse said, "Goodbye my friend. That's enough for me."

"What! Going so *soon?*" asked the town mouse.

"Yes indeed!" answered the country mouse. "Better bits of barley in peace than fancy foods in fear."

"To each his own," called out the town mouse as his friend ran away.

"Different strokes for different folks," called back the country mouse as he scampered into the woods.

Better bits of barley in peace than fancy foods in fear.

This fable is about some travelers
who listened to so much advice
they didn't know what to do.
Do you think they knew the saying,
Different strokes for different folks?

The Miller, the Boy, and the Donkey

A miller and his son were once
taking their donkey to market
to sell him. As they walked
along, they passed a group of girls.
Seeing the man and the boy walking
next to the donkey, the girls laughed.
"What fools you are," they cried. "Why
do you have a donkey if you don't ride him?"

So the miller put the boy on the donkey and
they went on their way. Soon they passed a group
of old men. "Look at that lazy boy!" said one of the
men. "He lets his father walk while he rides. Just what
I was saying. No one cares about old folks these days."

So the miller ordered his son to get off the donkey and
got on himself. They hadn't gone very far when they passed
some women and children. One of the women called out,
"Why you lazy old man. How can you ride while that poor
little boy walks? He can hardly keep up with you."

The kind miller wanted to please everyone. So he quickly
took his son up behind him. By now they had almost reached

the town. Then a townsman stopped the miller and asked, "Is that your donkey that is carrying such a large load?"

"Yes, sir," said the miller quietly.

"Poor thing. Why you two fellows are better able to carry that poor donkey than he is able to carry you," said the townsman.

"Anything to please you," said the miller and he and the boy got off. The two of them tried to think what to do now. They thought and thought.

At *last* they had an idea. They cut down a pole, tied it to the donkey's feet, and raised the pole and the donkey to their shoulders. Then they set off again for the market. Everyone who saw them thought this was such a funny sight that they ran out to laugh at them.

The poor donkey, who didn't like having his legs tied together, was frightened by the noise. Just when they came to the market bridge, he kicked loose the ropes and tumbled off the pole. In the struggle, he fell off the bridge into the river and was drowned.

The miller was angry and ashamed. Walking home slowly with his son he said, "You see, try to please all and you please none."

Please all and you please none.

21

The people in this fable were friends, or were they? That's the problem. What do you think about it?

Two Travelers and an Axe

Two friends were walking along a road together. Suddenly, one of them saw something on the ground and stopped to pick it up. It was an axe. "A very useful tool for chopping wood," he thought to himself. So he showed the axe to his friend.

"Look at what we have here," said his friend. "We have found a fine, sharp axe."

"Oh, no," said the first man. "Do not say that *we* have found an axe. *I* am the one who found this axe, not you. It is *mine!*"

So the two continued on their journey. Soon some strangers came running up to them. Spying the axe in the first man's hand, one of them cried, "Aha! That is our axe that you have. It is the one we lost. Give it back to us!"

"Oh, no," moaned the man who had found the axe. "Now we are in big trouble."

"Wait a minute," said his friend. "It is not *we*, but *you* who are in trouble. You did not want to share the axe with me when you found it. Why should *I* share the trouble it brings you now? After all, if you will not share something good with a friend, you cannot expect a friend to share something bad."

**He who will not share the prize
cannot expect to share the danger.**

Here is a fable about another pair of friends. One of them didn't know about the *Golden Rule.* It says you should do unto others as you would have them do unto you. See if you can figure out which friend didn't know the *Golden Rule.*

The Fox and the Stork

One day a fox invited a stork to dinner. The fox served her some thin soup in a very shallow dish. He could eat the soup easily. However, the stork with her long narrow bill couldn't find a way to even taste her soup. So she ate nothing at all and was as hungry at the end of the meal as when she began.

"I am sorry that you have eaten so little," said the fox. "Perhaps my soup is not tasty enough?"

"Not so," answered the stork. "I hope you will come to *my* house for dinner sometime soon."

24

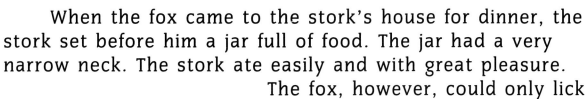

When the fox came to the stork's house for dinner, the stork set before him a jar full of food. The jar had a very narrow neck. The stork ate easily and with great pleasure. The fox, however, could only lick the rim of the jar and could get no food from it.

Watching him, the stork said, "See, my friend. I have learned well from your example."

Do unto others as you would have them do unto you.

The two animals in this fable make a deal.
Making a deal is like making a promise.
Who doesn't keep a promise in this fable?

The Wolf and the Crane

A wolf was gobbling some meat, when suddenly a small bone stuck in his throat. He couldn't swallow it and the pain he felt was truly terrible! When he could not stand it any longer, he ran from one animal to another groaning and groaning. He tried to find someone to take the bone out. No one would help him.

"I will pay you well if only you will take this sharp bone from my throat!" he gasped. At last the long-necked crane agreed to help.

"But before I try to help you," said the crane, "you must promise to pay me if I remove the bone."

"Oh yes, I promise. I will pay you," said the wolf.

The wolf opened his jaws as wide as he could. Then the crane put her long beak down the wolf's throat. She reached way down as far as she could

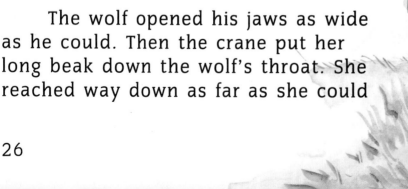

with her long neck to loosen the bone—and pulled it out. The operation was a success!

"You must pay me now, just as you promised," demanded the crane.

"*Pay* you? You ungrateful thing!" answered the wolf. "Your whole head was in my mouth. I let you take it out without biting it off, and now you expect me to pay you a bonus besides?"

Those who expect thanks from rascals are often disappointed.

People often say, *Never cry Wolf!* Do you know why? Read this fable and find out.

The Shepherd Who Cried ''Wolf!''

Long ago a shepherd used to tend his flock of sheep near a village. He liked to play jokes on people. He would pretend that wolves were attacking his sheep. He would cry out, as loudly as he could, ''Wolf! Wolf! Wolf!'' ''Help! Come quick!''

The villagers always did. Each time he cried ''Wolf!'' they dashed out in alarm. Each time they left with the shepherd laughing at them. Until one day, that is.

One day the wolves really *did* come and attack the sheep. The shepherd shouted and shouted for help. This time, no one came. The villagers, thinking he was up to his old tricks, paid no attention. The wolves ate up all of the sheep—down to the very last one.

A liar will not be believed,
even when he tells the truth.

28

Sour grapes! What does this saying mean? If you're not really sure, read this fable about sly Mr. Fox.

The Fox and the Grapes

A very hungry fox once saw some bunches of juicy grapes hanging from a vine on a hillside. The grapes were ripe and ready for eating. Being very hungry, the fox was ripe and ready to eat them. He leaped once, trying to reach the sweet fruit. No luck. He leaped a second time. No luck. He leaped again and *again.* No luck. The grapes were just too high.

When he saw there was no way he could ever reach the grapes, he gave up. He walked away with his nose in the air, calling out, ''Those grapes are sour and not ripe at all! I do not *choose* to eat them.''

Some people pretend to despise what they cannot have.

This is Aesop's famous fable about a clever, crafty fox.

The Fox and the Crow

A crow perched on the branch of a tall tree. He was just about to eat a tasty piece of cheese which he had taken from a window. A crafty fox saw the crow. He also saw the cheese and thought, "That's for me! I prize that cheese!"

Now this fox was very good at sweet talk and flattery. So he walked to the foot of the tree and spoke like this, "Sir Crow, how your glossy wings do gleam.

Your eyes are bright and sharp. Your claws are strong as steel. Your neck is so graceful. What a pity that you have no voice.''

''No voice!'' thought the crow, who had been thrilled to hear these wonderful words. ''No voice! I'll show that fox what this crow can do!''

''Caw! Caw! Caw!'' he screamed as loudly as he could and down dropped the cheese.

The crafty fox pounced on his prize and snapped up the cheese. Then as he ran off, he called out, ''Why, Sir Crow, you *do* have a voice! You have everything—except brains.''

Beware of one who flatters.

This fable starts
where the other story
about the fox and the crow ends.
It was written by James Thurber,
an American writer.

The Fox and the Crow

In the great and ancient tradition, the crow in the tree with the cheese in his beak began singing, and the cheese fell into the fox's lap. "You sing like a shovel," said the fox, with a grin, but the crow pretended not to hear and cried out, "Quick, give me back the cheese! Here comes the farmer with his rifle."

"Why should I give you back the cheese?" the wily fox demanded.

"Because the farmer has a gun, and I can fly faster than you can run."

So the frightened fox tossed the cheese back to the crow, who ate it, and said, "Dearie me, my eyes are playing tricks on me—or am I playing tricks on you? Which do you think?" But there was no reply, for the fox had slunk away into the woods.